John W. Wood

The Serpent Round the Soul

A Poem

John W. Wood

The Serpent Round the Soul
A Poem

ISBN/EAN: 9783337192822

Printed in Europe, USA, Canada, Australia, Japan

Cover: Foto ©Andreas Hilbeck / pixelio.de

More available books at **www.hansebooks.com**

THE SERPENT

ROUND THE SOUL:

A POEM.

BY

JOHN W. WOOD.

EDINBURGH: JOHN MENZIES & Co.
CUPAR: A. WESTWOOD.

1870.

PRINTED AT A. WESTWOOD'S STEAM PRESS, CROSS, CUPAR.

THE SERPENT

ROUND

THE SOUL.

Up from the waves the Sun rose red,
  To gild the Sabbath day;
The Winds came o'er old Ocean's bed,
  Low wailing on their way;
The Silvery Groves rang sweet and clear,
With notes that angels well might hear.

Yet lonely o'er the hills I trod,
  Long ere the chapel-bell,
With fervent spirit to my God,
  The ills of Life to tell—
When, as if God had leaned to hear,
The gentle breeze wiped off the tear.

A

Within that year my sailor-child
    Was lost, where icebergs roll;
Upon my ear his cries rose wild,
    That pierced my shattered soul;
While Memory would his form restore,
To leave me sadder than before.

To cheer the morn a stalwart swain,
    Came pressing through the broom—
With beaming face that well might gain,
    Dark mourners from the tomb—
And praised the Summer scene that lay,
So sweetly round our rural way.

Then come, he said, and spend the hours,
    Beside the tinkling rills;
Or list the music of the bowers;
    Or walk the heath-clad hills;
For Man may woo fair Nature there,
And find a balm for every care.

This heart was grieved, and pained this head,
    Within my native halls,
By a strange grief that daily spread,
    Like briers o'er fruit-tree walls—
I heard me of your Highland-side,
Where Liberty and Health reside.

And left the World's deceitful fanes,
  Where whining Priests may bow,
For Life now dances in my veins,
  Peace mantles on my brow—
And why should creatures of a day,
Not revel in yon glorious ray ?

The Christian.

Nay, nay, I dare not spend the hours,
  A holy God has given,
In plucking Earth's poor fading flowers,
  Upon the way to Heaven—
And soon yon Sun so round and bright,
Will set in everlasting night !

(Thus checked in sin, a flash of scorn
  Lit up his piercing eye,
As lightning, from the black cloud borne,
  Darts o'er the troubled sky ;
While mutterings presaged the storm,
That raged within the trembling form.)

The Stranger.

A God! away no one knows where,
  Watchful, and sad, and lone,
High-seated, in the realms of air,
  Upon a golden Throne,—
Go call thy wandering thoughts again,
From wildest fancy of the brain.

Than Nature! there is none beside,—·
  In vain you bow the knee,—
No Adam fell,—no Saviour died,
  For Sinners *such as thee!*
And where's the use your Christ should die?
And why God's mercy-price so high?

For if a Being good and wise,
  Would raise your fallen race,—
He had not claimed such sacrifice,
  The channel of His grace,—
Nor ever made you trembling slaves,
Hemmed in by gloomy loathsome graves.

Besides, it were too deep a bend,
  For such a lofty God,—
Too far remote,—too vile the end,
  Seen from a God's abode,- -
Degrading for One throned so high,
So erranded to leave the sky.

But ah! the Mind of wily Man,
   In search of Fame and Place,
Framed and enthroned with wondrous plan,
   A Godhead o'er the race,—
A Being with entire control,
Who moulds a World or breathes a Soul.

When, as they could not show their God,
   They placed Him far away,
In realms where mortal never trod,
   Or Nature found her way,—
Conceived the spheres of Fire and Grace,
And ours a fallen rebellious race.

The one wrapped in eternal night,
   Where tortured spirits roll,—
And one where unsurpassed delight,
   Surrounds the ravished soul,—
One yawning with wide hideous jaws,
The other closed with stringent laws.

Set o'er the Earth a monstrous Chief,
   Wily in vice and strong,—
To bring Mankind to direst grief,
   To drive fair Nature wrong,—
His only study that of fraud ;
His only joy, at war with God.

At war upon the heights of Heaven,
  Where squadrons charged and fell—
Now, since the fiendish host was driven,
  Downwards to Earth and Hell,
Within the hearts of men, and there
The old black banner beats the air !

Yet all the way from Heaven to save,
  Brought down God's only Son,
Who bled and died and found a grave,
  To raise you every one,
Up from the blazing mouth of Hell,
All of their slaves that don't rebel.

Those frauds in glowing imagery,
  By cunning scoundrels dress'd,
Were hung before the simple eye,
  Aroused the gentle breast,—
While Parents with a trembling tongue,
Enlarged and pressed them on the Young.

And still they tell them o'er and o'er,
  With sanctimonious drone,
While many light their foreign shore,
  By painting black The Known,—
When, as the people stay to stare,
It shews what piety may bear

The Christian.

(The Voice, that from my infant-day,
    Inspired my walk in life,
That through the desert leads my way,
    That shuns the haunts of strife,—
My "rest in God," my stay, my all,
Shall ye before this mortal fall!)

Cease reckless Man! your fiendish glee,
    And tell me if you can,
Who bade our World go rolling free?
    Whence sprang the race of Man?
What mighty Power? what God-like Eye?
Held watch beside the pregnant Sky.

The Stranger.

Yet add, a few more questions here!
    Whence came your glorious God?
Where is the Day-eternal sphere?
    Who waved the magic rod
To call them forth,—for you but dream
About a sourceless endless stream.

Who smote the rock with thunder-blast ?
  Who bade the stream arise,
Among the Life-hills of the Past,
  Across the gleaming skies ?
And how may such god-waves roll free,
Beyond Life's universal Sea ?

The Christian.

Nay, Stranger, nay ! keep 'neath the skies !
  How came the Parent-pair ?
Clods could not say, " let us arise,"
  To Manhood wise and fair,—
'Twere well to know of Mind and Matter,
Ere we would grasp The Great Creator !

And ere you prove to anxious minds,
  The orphanage of heaven,
Go pour your venom on the winds,
  That round the hills are driven,—
When, if ye find *Man* high o'er all,
Across your god-ship draw the pall !

The Stranger.

All right, my Friend, those Suns that loom,
 Have ever rolled through space,
For out of that no waiting room,
 Might hold them ere the race,—
From whose fierce wombs, like glory-rain,
Fly worlds that circle back again.

Creatures of fire, and of the wave,
 And of the stubborn clay,
Come in their time, and joy or rave
 Away their measured day,—
From the Life-caves, clan pressing clan,
From Salamander on to Man.

Millions of Beings crowd the air,
 Each sea, and hill, and plain,
Which go away in pale despair,
 But aye come back again,—
For all that hails from Life's bright shore,
Has lived ten million times before.

Lived in the unremembered Past,
 Within the early Seas,
The monsters slimy, dull, and vast,
 With undivided ease,—
Or as the vile unshapely host,
That crawled along the rock-bound coast.

Or by the streams and marshy plains,
    And in the tangled brake,
The terror of those bleak domains,
    Lay coiled the spotted snake,—
And who shall doubt each lying tongue
Is from such reptiles meanly sprung!

Or scampered o'er the burning sands,
    Or shook the desert air,
Or hunted in the fierce wolf-bands,
    Or growled within the lair,—
And Paul, the lecturer of men,
May once have graced the lion's den.

Or on the strong wing, rose away,
    As they had pierced the blue,
By silent night and solemn day,
    To distant regions flew,—
So much inclined to rise and roam,
That Earth might scarcely be their home.

Or when the vocal forest rang,
    Tuned by the wandering breeze;
Among the branches hopped and sang,
    In concert with the trees,—
The Notes of Nature sweet and clear,
As if a downcast World to cheer.

Thus *Change* is ever on the wing,
  In the eternal strife,
Of Mind and Matter ; *Chance* the king,
  Who calls the twain to life,—
While Death is nought but to unbind
The subtle fragments of the Mind.

Ever from Nature's myriad-gates,   .
  By wave or rushy lair ;
But no kind welcome ever waits
  The common creatures there ;—
They friendless come and spend their day,
And at night cheerless pass away.

But when Man, from the labouring ground,
  Gazed out upon the sky,
Surveyed the scenes that lay around,
  With wonder-stricken eye,—
The beaming Sun retiring, smiled,
As father o'er a darling child.

With a strange calmness on each face,
  The tribe of Man went forth,—
The first-spring of the noblest race,
  That ever graced the Earth,—
And clustering in a Summer dell,
The fruits and streamlets bade them dwell.

But the woods were not always green,
   And laden with good cheer;
Nor always through the sylvan scene,
   Ran streamlets smooth and clear,—
The howling Winter rushed amain,
And gloom sat throned on hill and plain.

Chilled in the scanty forest beds,
   When Winter's breath might blow,
They twined the wattles o'er their heads,
   To screen the drifting snow,
The northern winds, the sweeping clouds,
That drenched them in their leafy shrouds.

Yet pressed by wants, or urged by fame,
   They shaped their glorious way,--
The Sun of Reason upwards came,
   With Morning's genial ray,
Rose mantling o'er their stretching sky,
And lighted up each savage eye!

Gave names to beasts and all they saw,
   By which they should be known,
Until they framed, by pristine law,
   A language all their own,—
And mark, in that far night-seen ray,
The Sun that lights our mental day.

The children wandered down the vale,
  To spend the Summer hours,
The sweets of Nature to inhale,
  Among the fragrant flowers,
The leaf-arched streams to wade and trace,
With beauty mantling on each face.

And one day at their merry games,
  With wood-resounding glee,
They played at " swing " till out sprang flames,
  Where crossed the balanced tree,—
When flocked the old ones to admire,
And in deep wonder fed the fire.

One grasped the dancing nymph-like flame,
  To hold it from the sky, —
But curse soon thundered on the game,
  And anger filled his eye,—
Yet they its value came to know,
When Winter wrapped their Land in snow.

For when the Winter, in its ire,
  Came screaming through the door,
They circled round a blazing fire,
  That graced the wigwam floor,—
And when the blasts howled loud and long,
Their blessings flowed in mirth and song.

But coziness within the beild,
  Gave keenness to the blast,
So that they could not roam the field,
  While sullen Winter passed,
Till they had set the wily snare,
And trapped and skinned the monstrous Bear.

Then wrapped within the furry hide,
  Adorned with shining shells,
They climbed the mountain's icy side,
  And braved the wintry swells,—
Or o'er the hills on Summer morn,
Pressed all regardless of the thorn.

While further on, the Beaver Crew,
  Afloat with bushy tail,
Gave them to shape the rude canoe,
  And raise the driving sail,—
When, bravely, 'mid the dashing spray,
They bore to foreign coasts away.

Again, beside the desert stream,
  Nestled the little Bands,
Weaving, as in a happy dream,
  The pliant willow wands,
Ere round the caves, or hung to trees,
Fish-baskets dangled in the breeze.

Again, they stripped the bark of Pine,
    For fibres tough and long,—
And soon upon the baited line,
    Ran fishes large and strong,—
And later, cunning hands with ease,
Made nets to sack their River-seas.

Then, when the clear sun-jewelled sky,
    Bent down and kissed the wave,
The crews, with spirits wild and high,
    Streamed from their rugged cave ;
And soon they brought with flashing oar,
The treasures of the deep to shore.

Again, he bent the deadly bow,
    And showered the arrow-rain,
Till Man became the common foe,
    O'er mountain, wild, and plain,—
Leagued with the blood-hound ; from his view,
The tameless beasts in dread withdrew.

Then did the early Fathers join
    As one, the wide world o'er,--
One common range—their cake and wine,
    Piled in one common store,—
O'er them a simple Chief who drew
His laws from Nature—drew them true.

While Chieftian's Sons to Manhood grown,
 Set out with chosen Bands,
Earth's sullen solitudes to own,
 And change to living Lands,—
And thus they spread them far away,
Till wilder waters murmured " Nay."

In time far-stretching tribes were they,
 And happy homes of men ;
Smiled to the passing god of day,
 From fertile slope and glen,—
Yet to disperse those kindly Bands,
Gaunt Famine stalked among the Lands.

When with a Sense o'er all the beasts,
 As Matter yields to Mind,
To drag along their joyous feasts,
 They yoked the lower kind,
And o'er the desert roving Man,
Urged the romantic caravan.

Then with the Arts, fair cities rose,
 With all the pomp of Life ;
While foes at home, and foreign foes,
 Rose with the rising strife,
That pressed each toiling downcast clan,
Who urged in blood the Rights of Man.

Then men began to think of power ;
   Around each Native Throne
The brave youths flocked in danger's hour,—
   The battle-blasts were blown ;
And o'er once gay and peaceful Lands,
Rose Courts of Law, and Soldier-bands.

And when the shock of battle came,
   Those who had played high part,
Led brainless troops, by sword and flame,
   Up through some city's heart ;
Or passed among the hills by night,
To put a clan to death and flight.

Broad acres passed into their hands,
   As warriors of " the right,"—
The fair fields of the rebel Bands,
   As trophies of the fight ;
Then good things tumbling went one side ;
Then rose on wrecks our gems of pride.

Yet laurelled wretches, red with stains,
   Look back their ancient line !
Boast Royal blood is in their veins,
   And as young gods would shine,—
As if they did not plainly see,
Man as the fruit of one great tree.

B

And that those Lands and Titles high,
   Might be defended well,
Castles rose bristling to the sky ;
   Priests blazed anew their Hell,
For men, who recklessly would dare
Death's fateful volley, crouch to prayer.

Thus, stage by stage, through length of years,
   Came Man's transcendent state ;
A god among the gleaming spheres,
   A child of heartless fate ;
Thus, from a world's mysterious womb,
The tribes do in succession come !

—————

The Christian.

No, dreamer, no ! there was a time
   Of universal gloom,
When stars, and all of every clime,
   Slept in the upper room,
Safe folded up in God's embrace,
Ere the time came to furnish space.

With keen imagination go
    Back to that solemn Past !
See floods of heavy vapour flow
    On each careering blast !
Hear God's voice ring through unrealmed space !
See infant-worlds begin their race !

See wild confusion in the skies,
    While Ages roll away,
See Systems form by mighty ties,
    See Suns burst forth in day !
Till Worlds, all systematic driven,
Proclaim a mighty God in Heaven.

Say if the hand of Chance could roll,
    Those bright and ponderous spheres,
Keep all the Seasons in control,
    But for a few brief years ?
Could regulate and hold on high,
The wondrous clock-work of the sky ?

Could Chance have slipped them all away,
    With laws they must pursue,
Have poised them on their whirling way,
    To time and distance true ?
For one short instant fast or slow,
Had launched the sparkling host in woe.

And say if other than a God,
   Could, from chaotic space,
Have called those worlds that flash abroad ?
   And bade them run their race,— —
Or could with grand obedience given,
Have balanced all the Suns of heaven ?

See how Earth swings its way through space,
   With Seas that rave and reel,
While Masses move from place to place,
   Yet to the centre feel !
Then say who gives that inward force,
And that which rolls its circling course !

Look to the Earth's soft robe of air
   God flung, as round a wight,
To screen us from the Sun's fierce glare,
   Yet hold us warm by night,
Else all of life had stared in death,
With chilling midnight's icy breath.

Go mark the fierce volcano pour
   Its red destructive stream ;
See how its wide jaws gape and roar ;
   See volleyed smoke and gleam
From the great heart of Fire that cheers
The Giant's pathway 'mong the spheres.

See Vapours from our Seas arise,
 To roll to Seas again ;
Hear Winds burst wildly through the Skies,
 To press Earth's bridle-rein ;
Know Earth would from her pathway glide,
If other than a God were Guide.

Then search the forest, mount, and plain,
 Each stream, and lake, and sea ;
Mark how the tenants there maintain,
 Their kinds, by fixed decree ;
And say if Chance walks to and fro,
To bid those living streamlets flow.

Could Chance go god-like to a throne,
 To guide the surging throng ?
Collect and build the measured bone,
 Secured with muscle strong,
Erect the flesh-walls firm and fast,
A fabric that may brave the blast ?

Contrive the heart—the lungs—the veins—
 And bid the red stream roll,—
Fit up the head, and place the brains
 As lodgement for a soul,
Post the sense-sentinels around,
To guard the consecrated ground ?

Strange Sentinels that catch the tale
   Of love, or wrath, or woe,
That comes upon the idle gale,
   Or 'tween the fond hearts flow ;
And mark the working of that eye,
That bids the soul embrace or fly.

And who may tell how they convey
   The tidings to the soul ?
Or how the willing limbs obey
   The Spirit's high control ?
Nor think that clods may take in hand,
With schemes Man cannot understand.

Were all the life our isle contains,
   Nipped by a deadly breeze ;
Would e'er again from hills and plains,
   From rivers and from seas,
Spring up such forms they boast to-day ?
And cometh genius from the clay ?

Of olden times the fiercer beasts,
   That shook the echoing glen,
Have passed away in joyous feasts,
   To savage hunting-men ;
But praised be hill, and glen, and plain,
They never raised such breeds again !

Nor would it more bedim my sight,
  To see our monster hills,
Rise up on legs and speed their flight
  From Nature's numerous ills ;
Or see those worlds strong-winged arise,
And cleave their way through unknown skies.

While in the streams that streak the lands,
  Above the cascades high,
Save where borne up by sportive hands,
  No fishes charm the eye ;
Which proves, that water has no skill,
That all the Mould was God's great will.

But search with Fancy through the seas,
  For that god of your dreams ;
(The search how vain !) who gives with ease,
  Through all his unthought schemes,
The adaptation of those swarms,
To live in peace amid the storms.

Or if such power in Matter be,
  That it can Life descry,
The creatures of the land and sea,
  Ought nevermore to die,
Save, when they please ; else some great Power,
Away ! above ! must mark the hour.

And ah ! the Shakspeares of our world,
 Like echoes die away !
The canvas-mind be rudely furled,
 And whelmed in yon fierce ray ?
Our musings by the Summer streams,
And all our fonder ties but dreams ?

No, no, though from the fields of dead,
 New tribes of Earth arise,
The Spirits are for ever fled,
 To God, beyond the skies,
Working with Him for evermore,
New wonders on Heaven's blissful shore !

————

The Stranger.

But Sir ! the tale is more than queer,
 For any spirit-god
To will the Star-host to appear,
 And Life from lifeless clod ;
Strange that dull earth should hear His voice,
And in the shape of Man rejoice !

But wing your Mind for ever back,
  And watch the forming spheres,
And all the Beings on the track,
  To where lone God appears !
And say, must not He, if at all,
Have sprung with Nature's common call ?

Or in the awful solitude
  Of the uncheered expanse,
Have felt as in abandoned mood,
  Or dozed as in a trance,—
Spurned at a throne amid such gloom,
Ere Nature bade her flower-fields bloom ?

He fills, you say, the boundless space !
  Distant yet ever near !
Has not His throne upon the face
  Of some material sphere,
That angel-messengers might tell
Where The Great Father deigns to dwell.

But search the heavens all up and down,
  And no one meets the eye ;
No God sits there, with starry crown,
  O'er all immensity ;
No one is there to mark my prayers,
To pay my debts, or break my cares !

Brain is the only source of thought,
 Shape proves existence clear,
Limbs tell that action may be sought,
 Life moves 'twixt smile and tear ;
God hath not these, yet men will dare
To say He walks the lambent air !

And what the Being trod this earth,
 Or any other spot ?
Time kindly gazed upon his birth,
 And sighed " I know ye not,"—
And jeering Change will, day by day,
See gods and all things pass away.

The Christian.

Like thoughtless babe, you gather flowers,
 Upon Death's sunless hill ;
Your words imply still greater powers
 Than God more ancient still !
Gone back to Death, some great first cause ;
Blind gods endowing God with laws.

'Tis strange that He, The Great Unseen,
   Whom angels cannot know,
As God o'er all has ever been ;—
   Yet strange, and doubly so,
To come from Nothing's blackest shade,
Made up by Chance—from Nothing made.

But go a son of Adam scan,
   Your noblest powers unbind,
Pierce through the framework of the man,
   And paint the wondrous mind !
You fail ! then trifling mite of Time,
Sneer not at Zion's heights sublime.

While He, of Light, the Source and King,
   That fill'st the realms of space,
That flashest on the angel's wing,
   That beamest on man's face,
Walked forth, in heaven's full-glorious ray,
Ere worlds proclaimed our passing day !

Far in the spirit-world He reigns,
   Away from breezy hills,
Away from singing flowery plains,
   Away from gushing rills ;
For 'mong the stars, the proudest gem
May never touch His garment's hem.

Yet on the lone sea's swelling tide,
    Or 'neath the forest's frown,
Or by the loch and mountain side,
    When night is coming down,
The wanderer in humble prayer,
May meet his Heavenly Father there.

And if His mighty works be dim,
    If truth with strangeness blend,
Mark how your own will moves each limb,
    And plans each higher end ;
Where you may see, as best you can,
A little god within the man.

Yet gaze upon the glorious sun,
    Yon angel-eye so bright,
Round which obedient worlds do run,
    For Seasons, Life, and Light,
And bid your great immortal soul,
Around a " God of Mercy," roll.

Or when our earth has moved around,
    Gaze to the midnight sky,
All sparkling to the utmost bound,
    That artful tube may spy,
And think that He who formed those spheres,
The poor man's prayer in mercy hears.

Watch the vast comet flaming through
   The yielding crackling air,
To wondering worlds a striking view
   Of some rebellious heir ;
And say who guides its vagrant path,
And still withholds its awful wrath.

And think that up that endless sky
   Still worlds on worlds appear,
Bright flashing on the soaring eye,
   All glorious tier on tier,
Which round the dazzling rings are driven,
And light the countless plains of heaven.

Now all those worlds that pour forth day,
   Across each gleaming sky,
And worlds that roll their God-made way,
   With life-like harmony,
Shew plan, and build, and powers of light,
That speak of God's creative might !

Nor think that Man's poor boasted skill,
   The deeper ties may prove,
While all may see that some strong will
   Must make those worlds to move ;
The Spirit that first bade them roll,
Commanding still the glorious whole.

And were that mighty Will to stay,
 The countless throng were hurled,
Through waning realms with weird-like day,
 Fierce charging world on world,
Till vast Creation's restless frame
Rushed, dwindled, and dissolved in flame.

Give Fancy now a reinless sway,
 To chase those fragments on ;
Let countless ages roll away,
 Let untold space be gone ;
Grasp the case then, with whirling brain,
And learn, for Man to judge, how vain !

Reason's the insect of a day,
 When night is drawing nigh,
The sun is weakening in his ray,
 And Nature soon must die !
So are they blind, who walk abroad
To trace the footprints of our God.

Then mark the Seasons how they roll !
 And hail the coming Spring,
Its laughing suns, from pole to pole,
 Will make all Nature sing,
Mild airs come forth our earth around,
And flowers peep through the bursting ground.

Our horny-handed husbandmen
　　See gentle Spring has come,
That Winter's wild blasts have again
　　Gone to their icy home,
And in the providential plan
They haste to do the part of Man.

With joyful stir, the stables ring,
　　At early dawn of day ;
Out to the fields they blithely sing
　　Their sleek-skinned brutes away,
With their chains clanking as they go
To drag the ploughshare deep and slow.

And soon the straight-laid furrows gleam
　　O'er all the fertile plains ;
From man and cattle floats the steam,
　　That tells of faith and pains ;
The round-faced sun pours down his rays,
While birds o'er-head ring out their praise.

Follows the sower o'er the land,
　　His well-filled wallet bound,
With step precise, and measured hand,
　　Casting the seeds around,
Which soon must die, like sons of men,
To rise and bloom in life again.

Then comes the harrow rattling o'er,
  Closing the faithful scene;
But puny man can do no more,
  Than wait with trustful mien;
And, wicked man! dare you to found,
Your ardent hopes in that dead ground?

Up from the heated seas arise,
  Those clouds on airy wings,
That float along the stretching skies,
  Like armies led by kings,
Drop here and there the genial shower,
Till seems renewed fair Eden's bower.

The sun shoots down his warmest rays,
  With life to all below;
Around the earth the dew-shower plays,
  And healthful breezes blow;
Till man and beast rejoice again,
O'er waving fields of golden grain.

Not in the ground, nor in the seas,
  Nor in the beaming suns,
Not in the rain, nor in the breeze,
  Nor in air's thundering guns,
Is Power inherent;—but those cry
"O God but for Thee all must die!"

The Stranger.

My Friend! you very wisely said,
  Man may not read the stars;
We see them rolling overhead,
  A host of flaming cars,
But more we do not know, and never,
Though Man should gaze, and gaze for ever.

And as to fruits, blind Nature grows
  More weeds than golden grain;
Heather, and thorn, and tangled rose,
  On mountain brow and plain,
And, did Man say his toils were o'er,
Earth were a wilderness once more.

So far we see that Man must look
  To brawny arms alone,
To turn the leaves of Nature's Book,
  Her fruitage all his own;
And down to flesh should humbly bow,
Till spirits come to hold the plough.

You say that God makes all to grow,
  And therefore He is kind;
But men of deeper mind say "no!"
  For such one must be blind,
And worthy of our meek disdain,
Who sends us weeds instead of grain;

C

Who sees the toil-worn wight prepare
   The dull reluctant earth,
Bowed down with toil, and old with care,
   A common slave by birth,
Starv'd while he toils, and toil he must,
Till Death demands him to the dust.

The Christian.

This earth, Sir, when it teeming came
   From God's creative hand,
Was fair, as only God might frame
   A pure and weedless land ;
Whose God-obedient bosom bore,
Unhelped by Man, its ripened store.

A Paradise was hedged around,
   And in that sacred place,
God raised up from the silent ground,
   The Father of our race ;
O'er whom a deep sleep kindly came,
While God of one flesh formed the Dame ;

Gave them dominion o'er the brutes
  Of earth, and air, and sea,
Over the trees, to eat their fruits,
  Save sin's pernicious tree !
When this threat rang from bower to sky,
" To eat that fruit dooms man to die!"

Then roamed the pair by hill and grove,
  Or mused by lake or river,
From every breeze drew heavenly love,
  Lords o'er the earth for ever,
Walking with God, until their hand
Has stretch'd to break His stern command.

God-formed flower plots pleased their eyes,
  Fruits luscious round them grew,
Their ears bent ravished to the skies,
  Up heaven's long avenue ;
Then did the Senses sweetly roll
Their golden streams across the soul.

O ! third of all the happy states,
  Lords of a world all fair,
In sight of heaven's star-spangled gates,
  Beyond the reach of care ;
Who, battling the Satanic fires,
Had waked all heaven's admiring lyres.

But Satan serpent-guised drew near,
 Where Eve reclining lay,
And whispered in her drowsy ear,
 To cast restraint away,
Fly to the fruit, and Death defy,
For gods were never known to die!

To her pure breast he poured in pride,
 Her frail mind to elate,
Shewed her a throne, God's Throne beside,
 High o'er man's servile state,
Till all her feelings warmed to own
As gods, an independent throne.

Won o'er, she stretched her erring hand,
 The mystic apple ate,
Crushed with her heel God's first command,
 And lost man's happy state,
Came under power of fearful Death,
Whose nostrils held eternal breath.

Yet who may tell, if their canoe
 Had capsized on the river,
How wave-washed caves had pleased the crew,
 Till they got out, if ever,
How they had held unbroken dream
In the cold bosom of the stream.

But when they fell, they felt the shame
   Of nakedness and stains,
And dressed with leaves the lustful frame,
   A shame that still remains !
And ere you boast yourself a brute,
Cast off your man-adopted suit.

Pass through the crowds of staring men,
   Naked as ye were born,
Fling to each fellow back again,
   The burning look of scorn,
Dash from your soul the rising shame,
Ere brutedom may your body claim.

Then God drove out the fallen pair,
   And all their race ordained
To battle with a world of care,
   By sweating brows sustained,
Then all the laws united ran
To wildernize both Earth and Man.

Such labour not in anger sent,
   For through the deepest gloom,
When Vice would whisper ill intent,
   Or Grief would paint the tomb,
It leads the poor soul from the clod
To walk along the heavens with God.

While Sloth had oped the soul's front door,
   And waved wild passions in,
To caper madly on the floor,
   And raise the song of Sin,
Till Death should round the mansion creep,
And bid the soul for ever sleep.

Sin having forced the outer posts
   Of young Humanity,
The black Chief with his myriad hosts
   In Hell's black panoply,
Pressed onwards to each bristling mound,
Smashing Man's bulwarks to the ground.

All Hell was roused—the damnëd race
   Wore a terrific grin,
Close-watching Hope spread o'er each face,
   And lit the walls of Sin,
And raised her bastard feeble cry,
"The throne or may we doubly die!"

Envy, and Hate, and Murder came,
   As Man left Eden's gate,
With sullen eye, and knife, and flame,
   To crush his crumbling state,
And soon, were almost madly driven,
The holy spirits back to Heaven.

Unbelief placed false gods on high,
 As Races rose around,
Who pealed mad anthems to the sky,
 Yet down to earth were bound,
While Satan, proud to see each Race,
Leaned from his throne with beaming face.

Hypocrisy bade fiendish souls
 Stand up and rant and pray,
To hold aloft the holy scrolls
 That thread Life's tangled way,
For gold to shew the way to God,
Whereon their black feet never trod.

Vanity raised her luring shows,
 And Man from Nature drew;
Around the thousand stinging woes,
 Her gaudy mantle throw;
Drew "pious" Priests to tend the great,
And pass poor Lazarus at the gate.

Death oped with gruff unfriendly mien
 Eternity's grim gates,
Whereat old angels stern and keen
 Came forth to seal the fates,
And through the long dark Pass anon
A silent train is moving on.

High Pride, with strange unearthly airs,
   Led overbearing men
Out from their morning easy-chairs,
   Where both would be again !
To bid farewell to earth and sky,
For, with foul weapon, one must die.

Revenge secured the glancing steel,
   And bade assasins go
Close-muffled on the victim's heel,
   To strike the dastard blow ;
As if the malice of a heart
On streams of blood may best depart.

Robbery nursed her vile waylays,
   And scared the silent lanes ;
From cattled hills, and dreary ways,
   Drove forth the midnight gains ;
And told her lazy scowling bands
To live though blood may stain their hands.

Lust crept o'er Virtue's sacred wall,
   To scan the blooming bowers,
And with Love's mask thrown over all,
   Bears off the sweetest flowers ;
While parents hang their heads and rave,
To hide their grief within the grave.

Tyranny poured her fierce-eyed bands,
　　Forth from each pampered throne,
Who, with their blood-red dripping hands,
　　Reaped where they had not sown ;
And with the sword would point the way
To God's unending peaceful day.

War urged her hot-breath'd legions o'er
　　To fierce and.dauntless fields,
Mounding the earth with men and gore,
　　Weapons and broken shields ;
Blighting the gifts to Mankind given,
And all that makes Man kin to Heaven.

Yet, far upon the heights of Fame,
　　Men find a safe retreat,
Exulting in a warrior's name,
　　While blood-streams lave their feet ;
But they who fired the warlike train,
May cling around God's knees in vain.

Suicide, with sham sympathy,
　　Drove brain-bewildered men,
To fling back to the Deity,
　　His gift of life again ;
But who shall say they ring the bell,
And by the side-door pass to Hell ?

Old Age and Sorrow led men on
    With childhood's step again ;
Disease, with wasting frame and groan,
    Hurried her wrestling train ;
And forms, that now with beauty bloom,
Must sink again within the tomb.

Then Satan's loud artillery
    Confused the balmy air,
Rent the kind earth, and roused the sea,
    Till good men staid to stare,
And wonder why God gave him power
To change one floweret in His bower.

And then he brewed a spirit-flood,
    And filled his reeking bowls,
To nerve and keep in fiendish mood,
    The wild abandoned souls,
Who have renounced The Home on High,
And yet will curse their God and die.

Mercy, who whispered in the ear,
    Of Eden's parting twain,
To trembling saints drew fondly near,
    With words of love again,
That though " The Tree of Life " was riven,
There was a side-path up to Heaven.

Their souls revived, and sinking Hope
   Rose from her bended knees,
Seized Faith, as seamen seize a rope
   When Death is on the breeze,
And cried unto The Great I Am,
Who bade their beating hearts be calm.

The Stranger.

My pious Friend! and were you there
   To see those Scenes gone through?
Scenes, such as dreamers watch in air,
   To make priestcraft look true,—
You slept, Sir! as Time hastened by,
And know full well how men do lie!

And the same voice that calls them true,
   Should instantly inquire,
How God of Mercy stood to view
   The foul fiend, in his ire,
Wiling an inexperienced pair
To blast High Heaven's protective care.

How that He viewed on broad gangway,
    Up from the mouth of Hell,
The vile host press in dread array
    To crush what looked so well,
To plunge the coming race in crime,
To trace in blood the course of Time.

If such were damned—and damning all—
    'Twere meet they had been hurled,
So as to shun Man's dreadful Fall,
    Off to a distant world,
And that your Higher Powers of air,
Had kept them safely stationed there.

That Mercy, with love-swelling frame,
    Should drive such fiends again,
Back to the black sphere whence they came,
    No other worlds to stain,
Or all their stains should purify,
Or give them blissful leave to die !

To change the spears to pruning-hooks,
    To change the erring heart,
To cheer the bitter wayward crooks
    That mark Man's common chart,
To wipe the scenes of blood away,
The tears and strifes of sinful day.

To break the tyrant-chains that bind
   The humble o'er-toiled race,
To still the wild waves of the Mind
   That pale each honest face,
And crush all peace-destroying powers —
Were holy work for leisure hours !

And still inquire whence sprang that power,
   And whence such hate to Man,
That wings black Desolation's shower,
   And mars God's ancient plan,
When God made all things—made them free
From one touch of impurity !

Then hear each Sect attune the Psalm,
   And pour the peaceful Word,
Then turn and each the other damn,
   To glorify the Lord,
And mark how they in every age
Have stained the long historic page.

And one avers the world stood still,
   To let their fight be done ;
That God Himself was there to kill
   Who ever dared to run ;
And "held the candle" o'er the fight;
He stood so much up for the right.

Whose banner-bearers must not pause,
    Till o'er each land unfurled,
The glorious flag, that tells of laws,
    That ought to guide the world ;
Enough to make good men disown
The path that points them to a Throne.

But it shall never be Man's lot
    To live in love and peace,
Till he embraces fair Free-Thought,
    And superstitions cease,
When the unfettered mind shall roam
O'er earth as o'er a happy home.

The great Mahomet widely taught
    Laws straight from Heaven sent down,
And promised, that men might be caught,
    Each votary a crown,
To decorate their lovely heads
Beyond earth's everlasting beds !

When bands of blinded men came forth,
    With sanctimonious stare,
Believing that he had from earth
    A passage through the air,
Could mount his chariot, grasp the reins,
And roll along through God's domains.

Now that great chief you won't believe
  To be " God's only Son ;"
And where doubt is, babes may receive,
  While wise men will have none ;
For if a God would guide our way,
His star had blazed undoubted ray.

A voice as of a man had cried,
  And round the world would cry,
In words that could not be denied,
  From out the dark blue sky,
Unfolding Heaven's most holy will,
Pure as a streamlet from the hill.

But all the Mahomets and Popes,
  With all the wooden gods,
Hold out to trembling men fond hopes,
  To lead their future roads,
To where the sun for ever beams,
Fairer than Man can paint his dreams.

Who shall upon the latter-day
  High in these heavens appear,
While angels with their trumpet-bray
  Shall pierce earth's silent air,
And clear away the duller clods,
And wake mankind to meet the gods.

To meet the gods--ay meet the fiends,
  And ever with them stay,
For Mercy must remind her friends
  Of endless agony,
But what god ever could look well
Above the gleaming flames of Hell!

Now though the sweetest spot of earth
  For ever were your own,
Could you maintain the soul of mirth,
  Bid sympathy be gone,
If, from your lawn a stamped dog's cry,
Disturbed the sweet eternity.

Could One enthroned in majesty
  Look to the depths below,
Hark to the groans of agony
  That ring your place of woe,
Nor have His heart gush bounding free
To give the wretches liberty.

But how shall our long race arise,
  On " Resurrection day,"
When we, ere that time, to the skies,
  Have gone in gas away,
Have blazed and thundered through the air,
The elements nor will nor care.

Nor think the spirits of the dead
   Skim through the yielding air,
And, as young angels, ever shed
   On Man their utmost care,
For whither would such spectres fly
When howling storms disturb the sky ?

The Christian.

True, true, my very being lay
   In Nature's cold embrace,
And all those actors passed away
   Ere that I joined my race ;
But God's Will, to each soul is given,
Cut on the granite slabs of Heaven.

Our parents were not mere machines
   Moved by the Higher Will ;
Reason had they to grasp the scenes,
   To weigh the good and ill,
And teach Self-Love with gentle voice,
Within her boundaries to rejoice.

D

But "Fruits to be desired" were seen
　　Far in the higher states ;
Ambition stretched her wings serene,
　　Unmindful of the fates ;
And Reason fled her sacred post,
Else Paradise had ne'er been lost.

HE, who has marked the lightning's way,
　　And lulls it o'er to rest,
Or taught the linnet on the spray
　　To build her cozy nest,
Placed Man, where angels might have trod,
With all the freedom of a god.

He fell—and Memory's moaning stream
　　Pours its polluted wave,
Wherein thy deeds, as in a dream,
　　Do haunt thee to the grave ;
And say, for all your griefs and shame,
Was other than yourself to blame ?

Our metaphors bring up from woe
　　Fiends to attack our race ;
Hurry them o'er earth to and fro,
　　Like lions in the chase ;
But lost to Peace, they never roam ;
Fiends have enough to do at home !

And if the millions of our race
    Would spurn the Arts of War,
Would hurl down from each lofty place,
    And banish Pride afar—
Ten thousand sheaf-clad plains would rise
To wipe the tear from Hunger's eyes.

If they by Nature would abide—
    Their ball-room on the hills,
Their food as Nature would provide,
    Their liquor from the rills—
Health on the cheek of Man would bloom,
And check the eager gaping tomb.

After The Fall, our growing race,
    Fled from the Courts of Heaven,
Called God all names and spurned His grace,
    And would not be forgiven,
Till Order marked the mad display,
And vowed to sweep them all away.

As oxen freed from Winter-chains,
    Out to the Summer air,
With glaring eyes, and rising veins,
    Run madly here and there,
Man leaped each fence with fiendlike grin,
And revelled o'er the vales of Sin.

Yet there was one voice shrill and clear,
 Rang through the startled air,
With words of love that reached the ear,
 But strangely lingered there,
Old Noah to The Faith stood true,
Till God from Earth and Man withdrew.

To build an Ark, God moved his mind,
 His Family to save,
With numbers of the lower kind,
 Beyond the watery grave,
That would enwrap the wicked world,
Which had to Heaven defiance hurled.

Then—plank o'er plank--the Ark arose,
 Arose the scoffer's jeer,
Was he in dread of unseen foes,
 Or mad with pious fear?
And when the ship was built—in glee
They chafed him for his want of sea!

All safely stowed, and all shut in,
 The floods of heaven came down,
And seas gushed o'er the land of sin,
 The wicked bands to drown,
Up to the hill-peaks frightened crowds
Ran to evade their watery shrouds.

Then sounds of wild dismay came o'er ;
    Then arms were stretched in vain ;
While the huge Ark, with Life's small store,
    Rode o'er the raging main ;
Till the hills sank beneath the flow,
And wicked men slept sound below.

The dread work done—gone back the floods,
    From Ararat flocked down
The little brotherhood of bloods,
    The sin-rid world to own,
And bid earth bear her corn and wine,
And ring with birds and lowing kine.

Then Noah and his little band,
    Devoutly knelt to pray,
To Him who waves His unseen Hand,
    And winds and waves obey,
To Him who steered them o'er the wave,
That wrapped their kinsmen in a grave.

Then in the cloud God named the bow,
    To trembling Man a sign,
That angry waves would ne'er o'erflow
    A wicked world again ;
And that which once was but a span,
Now beams with mercy-rays to Man.

Nor do those thrilling Scripture strains
  Come to the test alone ;
Tradition cries from earth's far plains,
  From tribes till late unknown,
Whose rude prints shew a shoreless sea,
With Noah's great ship plunging free.

They tell, and tremble at the tale,
  That The Great Spirit flew
With water-floods, o'er hill and vale,
  And only saved that crew,
Of all the world-traversing throng,
As they had done some awful wrong.

Thus as from earth's bleak rugged hills,
  Shut out from kindly sun,
A thousand strong and tameless rills,
  In jarring accents run,
Meet in the vale, and join one course,
With friendly, calm, majestic force.

But Satan's never-winking eye
  Watched Heaven's high-favoured few,
And ere the flood-lands could be dry,
  His fatal arrow flew,—
For Noah cropped the good old vine,
And like old sailors took to wine.

He drank and laughed the hours away
   Without becoming care,
Till roguish Ham, one merry day,
   Came on him drunk and bare,—
And though I may not stain my page,
He earned the Great Shipmaster's rage.

For God loved Noah, and could feel
   How wildly he was tossed,
Knew that for long his steps would reel
   Upon the strange sea-coast,—
Till the ship's motion passed away,
He must have soothing grog each day.

When for his base unmanly acts,
   Accursëd was his line;
And on far Afric's scorching tracts,
   In slavery they pine,
A listless, helpless, Godless host,
In sin and degradation lost.

Nor to the first crime do we gaze,
   As the unaided cause,
Of the dark Afric's darker ways,
   For Heaven hath no such laws,—
But else, that bad examples pour
Rebellion to earth's farthest shore.

Now one had thought that favoured crew,
  (And generations more)
Whom God had watched the tempest through,
  Had clung to God ashore;
But through the growing race there ran
The crimes that seem as parts of Man.

While He, for whom all sacrifice,
  Was meant to typify,
Was hidden from their carnal eyes,
  In Heaven's unclouded sky!
While scorn and curse were heaped on those
Who saw the star-tints ere He rose.

God's name was scarce the world within—
  Yet in the dust they lay,
To move stone-gods for leave to sin,
  And sweep remorse away;
For, like all men who disown God,
They worshipped Man's most humble fraud.

But God's eye saw them, and His Will
  Went forth with God-like ire,
When down from the angry heavens fell
  Red streams of liquid fire,
Blazing Sodom and Gomorrah,
Filling Siddim's vale with sorrow.

And to this time the Dead Sea tells
　Of that terrific day,
Shewing that God can pour out hells,
　If Man can disobey !
Fit warning to each waif of Sin,
Fit foretaste of the hell within.

Still Satan saw a chance to reign,
　And smoothed their fears away,
Puffed up the wise (?) to make it plain
　That Nature's foot may stray !
And while the vale all hells outshone,
Men from afar sought God in stone.

While that the gods might still retain
　For Man a kindly mood,
Hordes of poor wretches oft were slain,
　As if they lived on blood,
With other honours meant to shew
Religious spirit down below.

Yet men from heaven barefooted came
　To those benighted bands,
Urged on their souls a nobler aim
　Than idols of their hands,
Shewed those gods had in times of ire
A bad chance with the fiends of fire.

That in High Heaven Jehovah reigns,
   The all-creating God ;
Laid down His laws—rewards and pains—
   And urged the righteous road,
As that which leads to peace alone,
Where strife and sorrow are unknown.

Laws which demand our endless praise,
   Praise half the age of God !
Which lead Mankind through Virtue's ways
   To God's divine abode ;
Dispel the gloomy grave-side fears
By glimpses of the far-off spheres.

Laws which the Wicked would not frame,
   And never would obey,
And given under that great name,
   The Good revere alway,
And dare not use in vain—shew clear
They were not, had not God been here.

Told Man to watch the unseen foe,
   Or dark would be his fate,
That Sin the Sinner would lay low,
   Outside Heaven's bannered gate,
That Sin would scatter nations far,
Upon the crimson surge of war.

And those great prophets told as well,
　A Saviour would be given,
Whose miracles alone might tell
　That He had come from Heaven,
Who in His own mysterious way
Would lead the tribes that were astray.

That though He came to grasp a world
　From out Hell's gaping jaws,
Would, while He Heaven's white flag unfurled,
　Receive no kind applause,
Would have to creep into a grave,
Within that world He came to save.

The Ages that must intervene,
　Had joined Eternity,
When the heraldic star was seen
　Slow floating o'er the sky, ·
Which led the wise men on the way,
To where the Infant-Saviour lay.

And men who watched their fleecy care,
　On Bethlehem's lovely hills,
Walked with strange messengers of air—
　And sat beside the rills,
In prayer to Him, who crossed and driven,
Would bring His Father's flocks to Heaven.

The Magi come to Herod's gates,
    Told they had seen from far,
As told by those who knew the fates,
    The bright heraldic star,
Of Him, The King of Kings to be,
For whom they searched to bend the knee.

Then Herod trembled for the throne,
    His foreign spears had won,
Called all his priests to make it known,
    Where lay the Princely One,
For he to bend the knee was fain,
To Him who would o'er Judah reign.

But not to priests, nor men of might,
    Did God His love declare ;
None but the wise men saw the light
    That slowly cleaved the air ;
And on they traced the bright star-track,
To find and fetch the glad news back.

But fast a-down the wondering sky
    From Heaven an angel sped,
And shewed them Herod's hellish lie ;
    The knife o'er Jesus' head ;
And urged the parents fast to flee
To Egypt, from the dread decree.

The dread decree through fear and rage,
    Which Herod rashly made,
To slay the babes of Christ-like age,
    Because those men delayed,—
Because his throne must firmly stand,
Though blood and hot tears drench the land.

When as if Heaven had found new foes,
    Which foresight scarce might tell,
A pack of fiercer fiends arose,
    Than ever peopled Hell,
Who killed the helpless smiling " Dears,"
And spurned the mothers' cries and tears.

Yet He who wings the surly blast,
    That snaps the stately pine,
Over the thrones of Mankind passed,
    To shape His great design,—
And Herod's arm that rose to slay
Was checked and changed to lifeless clay.

Then when the time-appointed came,
    Forth came the Saviour-God,
Preceded not by sword and flame,
    Bearing no " sainted " rod—
Came to unbar the gates of Grace,
As Heaven would yet receive our race.

Came as a sunbeam from the God
   Who flung the stars through space,
On to this bleak sepulchral sod,
   And mingled with our race,
To chase the glooms of Death away,
To cheer the souls with glorious day.

But such a King should not be theirs,
   And Hell within them burned,
And seemed to breathe within their prayers,
   While they that Saviour spurned,
Their trust was in a warlike train,
To hurl Rome's cohorts back again.

A King who would through War's red flood,
   Pursue earth's endless jars,
One who would pour the nation's blood,
   And ope the foemen's scars,—
And on they looked, and look in vain,
For one of earth to rise and reign.

Yet though they spurned Him from their sight,
   Or jeered His words of Life,
The same pale Preacher in His might,
   Gave kindness back for strife,
Spake, as ne'er man spake, pulling down
The gods of lust, of wood, of stone.

Told of a bright eternal Home,
    Where death and dust were never,
Where spirits in sweet converse roam,
    And feast on thought for ever,—
A Home whereof this hut of clay
May only catch the dust-dimmed ray.

Grasped not at earth's poor passing power,
    Bowed not to high estate,
Made no laws that the poor might cower
    Beneath a tyrant's hate,
Walked on the gilt things that the age
Had flung around the wily Sage.

Made deaf men hear, the blind to see,
    To sing for joy the dumb,
The lame to leap and dance with glee,
    Men from their graves to come,
Turning the rusted locks of clay,
As only God Almighty may!

Was followed by a faithful few,
    Whom kindness wrenched from woe;
Embraced and kissed by one He knew
    Would sell Him to the foe;
Was ever fiend of Hell so base
As try to cheat God to His face!

Whom had He waved His hand on high,
   With calm God-like desire,
Legions had rushed a-down the sky,
   To sweep the world with fire,—
But nay, He chose with Man to wail,
And place His lamp in Death's dark vale.

While had He been but Joseph's son,
   The gilded pomp of kings
Had made Him rush for Judah's throne,
   To taste earth's kindly things,—
March with tyrannic step through laws,
And list a Faction's loud applause.

Nor had He, face to face, with Death
   Maintained an aimless lie;
Nor had each follower's latest breath
   Proclaimed Him Deity;
For who would fill a martyr's grave,
An up-start god to guard and save?

Yet see Him led to Calvary
   To join with bloody Death,
And hear Him answer woman's cry,
   And with His measured breath,
Tell them to weep—but not for Him—
For Mankind and Jerusalem!

Yet see Him on the Cross of Pain,
   With slowly gathering tear ;
Mock-crowned with thorns in mad disdain ;
   Pierced with a coward's spear ;
And list to Nature's melting sigh,
While light flies hiding down the sky.

When as they raise their jeering shout
   Around the sinking form,
The flame divinest dazzles out
   Through Hell's collected storm—
" Father forgive these erring men
Who send Thy message back again !"

Ah ! Christ was of the spirit-sphere,
   Wrapped in our earthly form,
Through which the rays of Heaven shone clear,
   And fringed Affliction's storm,—
Passed through the tomb, and cleared the way,
For Mankind to eternal Day.

When as He sank beneath the sting,
   The Hosts in ecstasy,
Made Heaven's far-stretching arches ring,
   With sweetest hymns of joy,
For all of Heaven soon came to know,
That Christ had foiled Heaven's direst foe.

E

Again He rose above all men ;
　　Took rank as from the skies ;
When, to the crowds who jeered Him then,
　　And scorned His earthly cries,
He caused His first kind words be given,
To meet Him on the shores of Heaven.

Then the great scene that dimly sailed,
　　Before prophetic eyes,
Shone through the breaking clouds that veiled,
　　The pregnant future skies,
A painting true, of love and fraud,
To decorate the walls of God !

Well might angelic hosts, in awe
　　And wonder, downward lean ;
Well Nature might suspend a law
　　To hide the awful scene ;
Well did the Father from His Throne
Bend down and Christ the Saviour own.

Yet Satan and his host, three days,
　　Usurped the earthly throne ;
Stopped was the tongue of prayer and praise,
　　The world seemed all their own ;
But as the stars traverse the gloom,
He smiled and left the wondering tomb.

Came as " the risen Lord " to men,
  And rolled their fears away ;
In by the gates of Life again,
  In by the private way ;
When multitudes bowed down the knee,
Unto the God of Calvary.

Passed as a God the Roman guard,
  That paced the sacred ground,
When sights were seen, and voices heard,
  That all the watchmen bound,
Whom the vile Scribes had bribed to say,
They slept while Christ was stolen away.

Now mark ! He told them He would rise
  In three days from the tomb ;
The guard knew that for faithless eyes,
  Death was the standing doom !
With eager rage proud pomp looked on,
Yet with the third day Christ was gone.

When had He proved a wreck of clay,
  'Twere madness to suppose,
His followers would bear away,
  The cause of all their woes,
For had Death kept Him in his thrall,
All had been buried—Faith and all !

But take the case that such had been,
  While midnight veiled the skies,
That simple men had passed, unseen,
  A guard and myriad spies,
Some secret nook or ruffled ground,
Had whispered where he might be found.

Then with one touch of Deity!
  Burst forth a gleaming Light,
To cheer the heathen world that lay
  Without "a moon by night,"—
Lighting the tribes that far might roam,
Back to their God—up to their Home!

The great work done, He took His flight,
  Far through the star-thronged sky,
Escorted by the sons of Light,
  Up to His Home on High,—
Shook off the dust that earth might own,
Before He reached the Great White Throne.

Meanwhile the hosts in masses deep,
  O'erjoyed stood circling round,
When up the far and glorious steep,
  Their earnest gaze was bound;
And Heaven with all the Godhead shone!
And loud hosannas shook the Throne!

But Calvary's lights shone forth in vain ;
  The faithless tribe arose,
By force of arms to break the chain
  That bound them to their woes,—
O'er earth's low skies there passed a frown,
And all the lamps went hurling down.

While Titus with his warriors came,
  In terrible array,
A mighty host, with spear and flame,
  To hold a fearful day,—
When war-whoops made the land to ring,
And Death rushed forth on fiery wing.

When swept Destruction's awful blast,
  O'er earth's dark-fated land,
Dashing the grandeurs of the past
  From their rebellious hand ;
For fast before those fiends of Hell,
Their blazing cities crashing fell ;

When from War's groaning writhing bed,
  Arose the mother's prayer,
For mercy on the harmless head,
  But ah ! no God was there !
Nor infancy, nor bending age,
Could stem the wild unwonted rage.

Fierce curses raged from every tongue ;
    The massacres were dread ;
The heart-blood of the old and young,
    The reeking streamlets fed ;
While cornered wretches fought and raved
To clutch the morsel Hunger craved.

But darkest 'mid those scenes of blood,
    Where Hunger most oppressed,
The ravenous mother seized for food,
    The suckling of her breast,
The babe that in her face would smile,
And in Death's jaws laughed up the while.

Full soon their cities, bathed in blood,
    In smoking ashes lay ;
The fair land melted in a flood
    That scared retiring day ;
While they " the chosen " of the Lord,
In remnants fled before the sword.

While other conquered nations lose
    Their features and their line,
Within the glory of their foes,
    Nor wear subjection's sign,
They walk alone the Course of Time—
And Jews are born in every clime.

As prophets saw! that from their "hand"
   The sceptre would depart;
That they would roam through every land,
   Charged with a trembling heart;
Would walk as aliens round the world,
When they the rebel flag unfurled.

That tho' they spread thro' all the lands,
   Beneath the circling sun,
And mingled with earth's varied bands,
   They would belong to none,
That all the world with easy view
Might mark the wayworn wandering Jew.

And yet they hold the prophecies—
   Still for a Leader great,
They look with keen untiring eyes,
   To raise their earthly state,
Though eighteen hundred years have fled
Since the Messiah came and bled.

With facts so stern, who will deny
   The Scriptures are God's Word,
When wilds and ruined cities cry,
   "We own Thee blessëd Lord,"
When Nature gives her joyous shout,
Shall Man alone gaze on in doubt?

But soon the doubting wretch must stand,
   Before the judgment throne,
Dragged by a subtile unseen hand,
   Where he our God must own,—
Where he, bound down with Shame's black chain,
May plead his cause " for life " in vain.

And when the Sands of Time are run,
   Christ and His dazzling train,
Eclipsing in their flight each sun,
   Shall pass from Heaven's high plain,
To trembling earth with both the keys,
To bar the Two Eternities !

Then shall the Great Almighty Power,
   That formed at first our race,
Command the four Winds to restore
   Each fragment to its place,—
The Power that feeds earth's greedy urn,
Can surely bid such forms return.

(Ah ! while the dead flowers o'er my tomb
   Spring into life again,
Shall Sleep for ever be my doom,
   Shall Death for ever reign,—
Shall Spring-time for a floweret roll,
And be denied a priceless soul ?

But you, the Phenix-risen one !
   Of independent mind,
Should give forth orders from your throne,
   The pangs of Life to bind,
And force old ruthless Death to fly,
Because you have no wish to die !)

Then is the Summer of the Lord,
   When joys for ever bloom,
For those who died by flame and sword,
   By earth's tyrannic doom,
For all who kept the Faith on earth,
As their eternal only worth.

And then the Winter of the soul,
   With no returning Spring,
When, (as round Sinaï) shall roll
   The thunders of the King,—
When all the varied streams of Vice
Shall be locked up in chains of ice.

Then shall the Lost shed burning tears ;
   Each soul to madness driven,
Shall faintly hear, or think it hears,
   The Hymning Bands of Heaven ;
Shall gaze across the bleak domain,
Where Death, the living Death, shall reign !

Then shall they overwhelmed in sin,
   Call on the earth to yawn,
And take them soul and body in ;
   But when such hope shall dawn,
Earth and her hills with laughter rife,
Shall echo out the crimes of Life.

Each soul shall feel the awful frown,
   Which only outcasts feel ;
Shall fancy that all Heaven looks down,
   With strange satiric zeal ;
Yet blackest hearts shall ever dare
To wish their altered presence there.

Nor can we see that Justice veers
   In stamping self-made fates,
While those who have so tender ears
   Should mark the different states,
Brutes have not Reason for their guide,
Nor should be damned nor Deified.

The Stranger.

Men may, who closely watch the times,
　　Predict some startling things,
About the tribes of varied climes ;
　　The fall of states and kings ;
Or of a man, who would arise
To tell of homes, beyond the skies.

Which, when they so-far come to pass,
　　By twisting or by chance,
Men worship the prophetic glass,
　　While men-of-fancy dance ;
But Heaven or Hell ! no grief nor glee,
Till I be there shall draw from me !

For no one ever told me where
　　Our spirits live again,
When all the worlds dissolve in air,
　　Where Heaven may find a plain ;
How spirits live when passions die,
How laugh with joy or tortured cry.

Yet some men burst the common bars,
　　And soar on Fancy's wing,
Far up among the silent stars,
　　And meet Creation's King !
Walk through the halls not built of stone,
And count the gems that deck the Throne.

With more of impudence than awe,
　　Hark at the senate door,
While mighty angels pass a law,
　　For forces to explore,
Ere they for dire assault late hurled,
Take vengeance on this lower world.

Then shout that Man is all but lost,
　　Upon some desert plains;
That Hell has out a monster-host
　　To fill their dungeon-chains;
When, as old warriors raised their clan,
A thousand beacons blaze for Man.

And in our day they venture well
　　To trace each vast empire,
As if they rolled through Heaven and Hell
　　In chariots of Fire,
Whose writings one day by the sword
May claim the sanction of the Lord.

They tell that saints in Heaven gaze down,
　　With much anxiety,
On city, and on country town,
　　And on the rolling sea,
Smiling o'er friends on Wisdom's way,
And grieving o'er those gone astray.

That bands stand on the Heavenly shore,
 Toward their native land,
To meet the laughing friends of yore,
 With Welcome's kindly hand,
That all their heart-strings go full play,
While talking o'er earth's chequered day.

And blasphemous! place "Muirland Lairds"
 Beside "the Great White Throne,"
In loud praise of the vast "kailyairds"
 They proudly called their own,
Or crews of seamen wondrous vain
Of warships that had shook the main.

That families pass up and down
 The golden courts above,
White-robed and with a glorious crown,
 Harping the Songs of Love,
That thus they ever ever spend
The Summer Day that ne'er shall end.

Now such wild thoughts should lead your mind
 To doubt their happy Home!
Fond mothers who had left behind
 Sons who would never come!
Would dash their harps beyond their sight,
And join their sons in blackest night.

And all in Heaven had left behind
    Some friends of loving ties,
Whom startling scenes might so far bind
    The torrent of their eyes ;
Strange sight ! as deep the pale hands fling,
Fond tears were dancing on each string.

Nay more, the saints deformed on earth,
    High-backed or lank or lame,
Or walked the world stone-blind from birth,
    Or wore the bull-like frame,
Shall all pass through the faultless mould,
As Paradise could boast of old.

If such were true, men could not know,
    Though standing side by side,
Those who on earth were friend or foe,
    Stranger or love-allied,
Soul does not look on soul you say,
And God has changed the house of clay.

And it were well—for Country ties
    Would raise the vaunting cheer,
When host on host would keenly rise,
    And though nor gun nor spear,
Heaven were a Hell from shore to shore,
And "Scots wha hae" were played once more.

Now why not carry out the jest
   By cunning heads begun ;
Flash o'er the Mind with lively zest,
   A state of frisk and fun ;
When Reason from the great mass cries,
To learn the pleasures of the skies ?

Sound in the terror-stricken ears,
   As from " the God on High,"
What would dispel the grave-side fears,
   Make Mankind wish to die,
That Heaven will only shut out Sin,
That all the joys shall enter in ;

That rows of harpers thousand strong,
   Shall raise heart-soothing strains,—
That dancers shall not think it long,
   Nor be disturbed with pains,
But dance for ever, high and dry,
In airy halls beyond the sky ;

That sportsmen with bright.flashing guns,
   Aback the fleetest steeds,
Shall tear along most brilliant runs,
   With hounds of purest breeds,
Up glens and o'er the heights of Heaven,
Through the long day that knows no even,;

That glassy lakes shall stretch away
  Alive with pleasure boats,
That artists on the banks shall stray,
  'Mong groves and charming notes,
Taking the scenes that glad the eye,
For Heaven's great picture gallery ;

That hearts shall glow with fervent love,
  Without earth's crushing cares,
Enraptured o'er the realms above,
  Shall pass in happy pairs,
And even say there might be given,
Old-Sarah-like fond births in Heaven ;

That cricket matches shall be played
  Upon the glistening plains ;
That race-horse power shall be displayed
  By steeds with flowing manes ;
That all the plains shall sounding be
With happy bands in playful glee.

Yet, as such dreamers have not been,
  From earth and back again,
'Twere best to wait each coming scene,
  Where God—where Sin might reign,
For at the best man cannot say,
What pictures load the coming day.

Nor can I see that any Power,
  Could give a sure decree,
Could stretch into the future hour,
  And grasp what has to be ;
To be, has yet to take its form,
And may be sunshine—may be storm.

Before the first globe had been planned,
  (And it was planned you say)
And like a good ship fully manned,
  Slipped on its glorious way ;
The fair sight, could it well be known,
By Him who sits on Nature's Throne ?

Nor can the working of my mind
  By outward Powers be seen,
To every thought all gods are blind,
  Save through a willing mien !
And if they dwell in some far state,
How can they rule or know my fate ?

All is a secret, all a dream,
  To which I would not bend,
Which e'en Religionists do seem
  Too weak to comprehend ;
Yet shallow minds do venture far
To find God's uncreated star.

F

I've heard an old wife meekly say,
 That up beyond our sky,
God's Palace stretches far away,
 And is three storeys high,
That Paul was there, but took a vow
To keep the grand scenes from us now.

She seemed to see the little King
 Pass up the winding stairs;
To hear Heaven's joyous belfry ring,
 That lulled his earthly cares;
To see him stare, and hear him vow,
While perspiration damped his brow.

And all her hopes were pointing there,
 And ever down she knelt,
For in the yet uncertain glare
 Her kingly Saviour dwelt,
He who would stop the lion's roar,
And bid Peace reign from shore to shore.

Now Christ has come, yet quarrels rise,
 And nations pour their blood;
Men only call more to the skies,
 To stem the crimson flood;
But who in all the heavens might hear,
And would not break the bloody spear?

Who "shrined in Mercy" could behold
   The spite of Pride and Power,
Borne on by warriors fierce and bold,
   Burst in an awful hour?
Or could traverse the bleeding plain,
And pass unmoved the heaps of slain?

Who but a wretch of crimes and wiles,
   That "Hell" could scarce disclose,
Could loiter near the smouldering piles,
   Where cities proudly rose,
And smile to see a ruined land,
And hold and nurse the blazing brand?

Who with a heart whose love-strings thrill
   For "grief that's not his own,"
Could wander when the night is still,
   Near wailing homes and lone,
See mothers for their slain sons sigh,
Nor spare a tear to moist his eye?

Then mark the elements that rise
   And sweep the world around,
No god seems floating in the skies,
   Nor through the depths profound;
With dead men's bones the seas are white,
And earth rolls howling through the fight.

Now when strong waves the barque o'erwhelm
　　On wild and lonely seas,
Why does not God's hand grasp the helm,
　　And give the sailor ease ?
He who once calmed the stormy wave,
To save Himself, should others save.

Ah ! spurn, as should be spurned a foe,
　　Imagination's god !
Fair Freedom's trumpet loudly blow

　　O'er all the world abroad !
Give Sense and Passion fullest sway,
And raise to Man Life's happy day !

Without a god, a priest, a king,
　　We had few other ills ;
Excursion bands would gladly sing
　　Among the Summer hills,
Kept by the piles of gold that go
To move the prayer and raise the foe !

The Christian.

But mark, the ancient sacred page
    Proclaimed a Saviour-God,
Where Truth stood wrestling with each age,
    Till He earth's desert trod,
Who preached and died our state to raise—
A very God in all His ways!

Unlike the Màhomets that rise,
    Half-mad or with an aim,
Who seize the message from the skies,
    Yet Lust and War proclaim,
As if Hell baffled would pluck down
The thorns she plaited for His Crown.

Nor did the heavens fall down to earth,
    When God reached down His hand,
But rose as rises earth-born worth,
    When one, who might command,
Tends the poor man who sickly lies,
Beneath the cold unfeeling skies.

But if you will shut up the doors,
    And hold yourself apart,
The stream of Grace but idly pours
    The balm that cheers the heart,
The soul that might have worn a crown,
Must to the brute sink coldly down.

Nor shall the Scriptures fall or rise
　　By rash aspiring men,
Who push Conjecture up the skies,
　　Beyond dull mortal ken,
For there to humble Man is given,
In lowly phrase, the Will of Heaven.

Yet, as the larks, that singing soar,
　　In search of milder skies,
We love the souls who meekly pour
　　Their Heaven-fraught melodies,—
Who 'neath the cold clouds will not stay,
Who with the Morning soar away.

Who, to the highest bars, ascend,
　　By sweetest impulse driven,
From this suburban scene to bend
　　Toward the walls of Heaven,—
As captives gaze the blue sea o'er,
With fond thoughts of their native shore.

And spurn the sparrows of our race,
　　Birds of a wintry clime,
Who leave no soul-inspiring trace
　　Upon the sands of Time,
Who sit with closed and dwarfish wing,
Who will not soar, and will not sing.

While he who gives a willing ear,
    A true confiding heart,
Thinks on his God with holy fear,
    And steers by Heaven's great chart,
(Writ on the everlasting soul)
Is happy tho' Life's billows roll.

But mark the man, the tribe mark well,
    Who fling the chart aside,
Who own no God, and fear no Hell,
    Who go forth in their pride—
Wild passions drag them roughly down,
Debasement marks them as her own.

Nor will Almighty God divide
    Into a thousand forms,
To watch and wander far and wide,
    To quell all rising storms,
To steer your boats, and sharp your ploughs,
To burst your guns, and break your bows.

For God would be a God no more
    In such ignoble course ;
For Man's Estate were toppled o'er
    If he were ruled by force ;
And for each stab, and for each groan,
Man is to blame, and Man alone !

God framed the worlds and set them laws,
　And well those worlds obey;
But little Man would know each cause
　In all his Maker's way,
And where he may not see or feel,
The daring wretch would set his seal.

While if he would his own frame view,
　Its functions part by part,
And watch the spirit gazing through,
　And hear it damn Chance-Art;
That Conscience with a fiery tongue,
Might rise and cry " From Greatness sprung."

For oft as I would grasp and know
　The inmate of my breast,
Down to the dust I bend me low,
　With ignorance confessed;
I am—yet I am all unknown,
While I "the God of Hosts" must own.

Now fancy how a man should be
　Unto himself unknown,
Yet dare the Heavenly State to see,
　And grasp God on His Throne
Because He fails him, flings aside,
God and the common truths beside.

Without a God, earth were a blank,
　　A cloud hung o'er each day,
The pretty flowers were dull and dank,
　　Yon sun of gladdening ray,
A tyrant marking out our doom,
A tyrant pointing to the tomb !

Without a God, the secret paths,
　　To where poor sinners fly,
For refuge from the common wraths,
　　Communing up the sky,
Were but the gloomy lands of Death,
With rankest poison on each breath.

Without a God, this little life
　　Were but a passing gleam,
Gilding the deep dark clouds of strife,
　　To shew the horrid dream,
And darker paint the coming state,
Destined to swallow all of great.

Without a God, earth were a hell—
　　For all Man's noblest powers,
Had occupied a narrow cell,
　　Within the passing hours ;
And Strife, and Hate, and Lust, and Blood,
Had raised a race-o'erwhelming flood.

Without a God, our thoughtful race
　　Had wandered on in tears ;
No smile had ever cheered their face,
　　Nor music charmed their ears,
Nor sweet companionships had been,
To wile away the short-lived scene.

Without a God, when dangers rose,
　　Or stinging Sorrow pressed,
The man bowed down by crowding woes,
　　Which earth had ne'er redressed,
Had plunged through Time's partition wall,
To sleep in Death's oblivious hall.

Without a God, how cold and dread
　　The thought had crossed the mind·—
Deep in this earth shall be my bed,
　　Each fond tie left behind,
My spirit and my frame-work gone
To dark and cold oblivion !

Without a God, yon beaming sun
　　Had blazed himself away,
His friendly orbs had ceased to run,
　　Enamoured of his ray,
And straight through never-ending night,
He had pursued his cheerless flight.

Without a God, the rolling sea
　　Had never yet been bound,
Its dark blue waves all bounding free,
　　Had wrapped the world around,
But ah! without a God of might,
Space had been one eternal night.

And as the magnet ever turns
　　Towards its native bed;
As heart to heart that fondly burns,
　　By unseen ties are wed;
As guide-flowers on the prairie wastes,
Wheel with the sun as round he hastes.

So all our thoughts by day and night,
　　Electrical flow out;
Earth's portrait on each ray of light;
　　Each whisper as a shout,
And in clear waves glide smoothly forth
To God, as wheels the needle north.

Thus are the Records kept by Heaven,
　　Which ever roll away,
And though to men they are unseen
　　Upon the darting ray,
God's burning microscopic eye
Can read our actions in the sky.

Which, if you doubt for want of sight,
  Just change the present scene—
Descend Life's scale to starless night,
  Where you perchance had been,
Where brutes in vain would spend their span
To grasp the mind of mortal Man.

Or search Wielieska's dark salt mines,
  And find old natives there,
O'er whose long night the dull lamp shines,
  Their only sun and fair !
And learn if language can convey
The richer scenes of glorious day.

To that deaf man go forth again,
  On whose ear sound ne'er fell,
And mimic Music's cheering strain—
  Its grand majestic swell ;
Nor yet expect with all thy art,
To rouse the feelings of his heart.

So are the heavens above us all,
  And he who would know more,
Shall drift within a dreadful squall,
  Along a starless shore,
Where black rocks rise, and wild winds waft,
To sink the puny, daring, raft.

* * * * * *

Then bell chimes called to holy men,
　　From out the fitful breeze,
That scoured the hill, and swept the glen,
　　And sighed among the trees,
While solemn flocks released from care,
Poured in to meet their God in prayer.

Round in the churchyard was the stand,
　　Where brave old worthies shone ;
And there he grasped each friendly hand,
　　Knew all, yet was not known ;
Passed o'er the tombs with sacred care,
For " dear old friends " were lying there.

Hinted they buried far too deep,
　　Who wished their friends to rise ;
That tho' they wakened from their sleep,
　　They could not reach the skies ;
And it were sad to wake to pain,
Remember life and die again.

The last peal like an angel stirred
　　The wanderer of night,
Who said he dared not meet my Lord,
　　Unless I spared his mite,
For now, he said, " the house of prayer
" Brought out ' the golden calves ' to stare."

When in we moved with solemn pace,
    And climbed the pulpit stair, ·
For he would see Man face to face,
    Each saint and sinner there—
Whom if he gave some saints their due,
They almost made him worship too.

Soon ill-bred eyes began to scan
    That face they " ought to know ;"
While thus their twitterings mostly ran,
    " Who's that with So-and-So ?"
But none in all the parish knew
Their dark complexioned friend in blue.

From pouch he pulled a parchment long,
    And crossed his stately knee,
Which made me think he'd argued wrong,
    My depths of Faith to see ;
Yet glad was I if he would scroll
God's living letters on his soul.

All in our seats—and silent all,
    The grey haired pastor rose,—
To Heaven's gate went with humble call,
    Then for a text he chose,
" Creation, and its boundless plan,
" And God's eternal love for Man."

Soon as the pregnant text was out,
  Some leering faces met,
To shew they had some clever doubt,
  And saw each way a net;
Some of those grave men and profound,
Who crawl like moles beneath the ground.

And he began :—Small Mind is prone
  To judge of God by Man;
Of Heaven's as of an earthly throne,
  And say His work began;
Creatures who once thought Earth a plain,
And feared of tumbling o'er the main.

Because that they themselves were born,
  And hasten to their close,
They feel that on some far back morn,
  Those worlds from Nothing rose,
That ere that time, or something more,
God never saw a world before.

But as the fountains gurgling rise
  Among earth's myriad hills,
Rush to the seas, and climb the skies,
  Whence water back distils—
So do the worlds dissolve and form,
In one eternal round of storm.

And as they hiss and blaze along
   Through Friction's fiery pass,
As from the gaseous state they throng
   Up to the solid mass,
All Life must perish, and they rise
Like unmanned ships across the skies.

Here God Almighty must put forth
   His strong creative power—
Fling germs across the maiden earth,
   And term the sheen and shower,
And above all bid Man appear,
With all the laws that bind our sphere.

Here the first link of earthly things
   (Oh! blessèd high belief)
Hangs on the holy King of Kings—
   Creation's glorious Chief;
And he, who will not find it there,
Should tell his fellow mortals where.

Men quarrel with the Age of Man,
   In tumults to and fro,
As if our *parents* lived more than
   Six thousand years ago,
But who can, tho' it were unfurled,
Go read the dial-plate of a world.

In Rock-formation there appears
　　Strange influence at play—
And that which takes a length of years,
　　Accomplished in a day,
Is in some famous Irish stream,
Upon the sunken forest beam.

But other than those lights that roll
　　Across those glowing skies,
Must fall upon the earth-born soul,
　　Ere it in triumph rise,
From doubts and terrors that assail,
And make the strong man shake and quail.

Kings of the earth have sought for Peace,
　　Within their vast domain,
But as the red sword gave increase,
　　They saw their wish was vain,—
For the grave frowned, and even kings,
Must vanish with the wreck of things.

Statesmen who framed their country's laws,
　　By lives of toil and care,
Have walked amid the loud applause,
　　And fondly sought it there,
But when the sweet sounds died away,
The soul sank down upon the clay.

G

The poet on his moss-grown seat,
  Beside the waterfall,
Would fondly all his sorrows cheat,
  And fain forget them all,
But with the falling of the leaf,
His lonely heart breaks forth in grief.

And ev'n the warrior would find
  It 'mid the battle's roar,
Or on the after-puff of wind,
  That bursts from shore to shore,
But each brave scene goes fading bye,
Like mist upon a wintry sky.

All classes of Mankind have striven
  Upon their various way,
And all went groping far from Heaven,
  To catch the peaceful ray,
But the Christian, and he alone !
Finds Peace, with God's Word, at the Throne.

He sees a Home beyond the grave,
  A Home beyond the sky ;
A strong Hand ever stretched to save,
  When Nature's form shall die ;
While in the jaws of Death he hears
The peaceful streamlets of the spheres.

Yet thoughtless men would earn a crown,
　　By sending Peace away,
Would with remorseless hand pluck down
　　The Sun of Life from day,
And leave poor souls in piteous plight,
To lose their way in darkest night.

Again some men would raise the cry,
　　That God must be unjust,
Unless He leave the souls to lie
　　Within the dormant dust,—
Of which is Hell—and curse the hour
They fell into such monstrous power.

And grumble at the strange foresight,
　　As if He sent to Heaven,
A band led there by Heavenly Light,
　　And others Light ungiven,
Away to hells of wrath and storm,
For sins He doomed them to perform.

Who cry "we need not strive to gain
　　"Those pleasant heights of Heaven,
"God doth the different states ordain,
　　"Whatever is is given;
"If Hell be ours, we there must pack,
"If Heaven, no sins will hold us back."

As if they thought that God would vent
  His wrath on petty man,
As if they grasped the full extent
  Of His eternal plan,
As if they knew how Man could fall,
Or how there could be Hell at all.

While *foresight* doth not interfere,
  To mould and cramp the will,
Till all the sons of men appear
  Mere waifs of good or ill,—
For Reason points the living way,
And Free-Will may or not obey.

Thoughts of the basest acts might flash
  Across a sinless mind,
But Reason, with an ample dash,
  Leaves not a trace behind,
True as the sun, the beaming soul
Shoots up to Heaven though clouds may roll.

But no one ever scaled the skies,
  When Chance prepared the wings,
Lost in the wilds of Sin he flies,
  Who spurns the King of Kings—
The Sun of Life might cease to glow,
If blind Fate marks for good or woe.

Yet in God's Word is mystery,
    A "tree of Knowledge" still,
And much we err, when we would pry,
    With weak and fettered will,
Among the silent leaves that spread,
Around and cool the sainted head.

But there the stream of Heavenly Grace,
    Through Time's vale calmly flows,
In whose waves all of Adam's race
    May plunge from sins and woes,
Whiche'er at times, or dull, or dry,
We trace its waters from the sky.

O! God look through Thy mask of stars,
    On those who spurn Thy Grace,
Ere Death shall burst their mortal bars,
    And wing their souls through space,
Draw them with bands of Love, to bow
Before Thy Throne of Mercy now.

And on he went in fervid strain,
    And stamped his earnest feet;
While yet my Friend's pen went again
    Across his crowding sheet;
When kindly feeling o'er me stole,
To know the notes that soothed his soul.

With sidelong glance, and stretching out,
 I read his graphic scrolls,
But horrors! they were all about
 Our poor rebellious souls,
As if our secret thoughts lay bare,
Each rebel to the Lord was there.

Those who would charm the Heavenly Throne,
 Yet win their neighbour's praise,
Whose earthly pride unwinged the tone
 They vainly thought to raise ;
For ev'n the music of the Fair,
Unhallowed may not enter there.

Those in gay Fashion's robes arrayed,
 Dressmakers and their friends,
Who, while the good old Pastor prayed,
 Made many awkward bends,
To see what this and that one wore—
How sat the work of weeks before.

The envyings that crossed the mind,
 The curl that marked each nose,
The spite that followed fast behind—
 As if a little rose !
Stuck neatly on a thoughtless head,
Should raise church-demons from the dead.

Those men who walk the world as lords,
   With grasp on earth and sky;
Whose slaves must load their groaning boards,
   Though slaves of hunger die;
Whose door swings harshly in the face
Of the poor outcasts of their race;

Whose Faith deep buried in their lands,
   Sound as a dead god lies,
Who trust to Chance, and toiling hands,
   To make the harvests rise—
Nor as they were but guardians high,
To deal the mercies of the sky.

The fireside, vast, heroic men,
   Whose dreamy daring minds,
Call clansmen from each hill and glen,
   And scatter to the winds
Our foes—with *me* to rule the force,
Deep-seated on the black war-horse.

The grasping half-starved miser kind,
   Who brooded o'er their store
Of hidden trust—and vexed the mind
   For more and ever more!
Who give their best days to obtain
What they must one day lose again!

The reckless gamblers fired with wine,
  Who, when the thoughtful train,
Had ventured o'er Time's hazy line,
  And on to Heaven's clear plain,
Upon the consecrated swards,
Shook out their dice and spread their cards.

Those glowing, merry, bright-eyed youths,
  Who for the earthly loves,
When the priest told of Saving Truths,
  Sped to the Summer groves ;
And when Affection bound the pair,
Sighed and saw all their heaven there.

The vain who boast of purer blood,
  Shrink from each ill-starred brother,
As if they do not at the flood
  All find a common mother,
As if there will to some be given
To have their cushioned seats in Heaven.

As if a little gold and lace
  Should give a grand control,
In and around the spheres of Grace,
  O'er each ungilded soul,
As if proud Fortune's passing blaze
The stature of the man displays.

Those who were drunk the night before,
 And cursed their zig-zag way,
Or dreamed they drove a coach-and-four,
 While in the mire they lay,
Who beat their wives, and frown, and swear,
Yet meet to call God "Father" there.

And on it went, and at the foot
 Ran words of fiend-like note—
"So far as I may now compute,
 "Earth's crimes may sink my boat,
"But all's well if there runs no gale,
"And I in good day-light may sail."

One moment, and my troubled mind
 Was overwhelmed in awe,
One moment, and upon the wind,
 Old Satan's form I saw!
The kirk and all went whirling round,
And in a swoon I clasped the ground.

Sudden arose a phantom sea,
 And howled a dreadful gale,
And from a weird-like shore full free,
 Bore on a ship full sail,
And my dark Friend stood at the helm,
Through seas that dared the ship to whelm.

Bloodshed and all the darker crimes,
   Mingled with formal prayer,
Tyrants and murderers sailed to climes,
   That God alone knew where,
And loud their howlings rent the sky,
Whene'er the ship went rolling high.

He had come round with seaman-glee
   To find a crowded ship,
But only hundreds could I see
   Among the waves to dip,
Of all Mankind ; yet blessed his pains,
While Judas lay aboard in chains.

Wilder and wilder rose the waves,
   The farther from the shore,
And as they yawned like living graves,
   The helmsman laughed the more,
And when the sick sang hymns for Grace,
Laughed till the red came in his face.

Some thought God had forgetful grown,
   And deep they drank and swore,
Till Madness sought to hurl the throne
   Down to the dismal shore—
When Satan through a fog so snell,
Told them the sea was rough to Hell.

Whereon the wretch that stabbed our Lord,
  Would put the ship about,
Came rushing with a naked sword,
  And gave a rebel shout—
But Peace was soon again restored,
And th' Roman was flung overboard.

Then Satan waved a fond farewell,
  For ever and for aye,
And I thought the parting quite as well
  For I love him far away—
Yet may the same good feelings be
In Time and through Eternity !

FINIS.

PRINTED AT A. WESTWOOD'S STEAM PRESS, CROSS, CUPAR.